I belong to

_____

D1120001

For my family and friends, including my little brother Adam.
Thank you for keeping me company on life's unique path.
–B.D.

Copyright © 2011 Brianne Drouhard.
First hardcover edition published 2011.

inspiring a world of imagination

Immedium, Inc.
P.O. Box 31846
San Francisco, CA 94131
www.immedium.com

All rights reserved, including the right of reproduction—in whole or in part—in any form.
For information about special discounts for bulk purchases, please contact Immedium Special Sales
at sales@immedium.com.

Edited by Don Menn
Design by Stefanie Liang

Printed in Singapore
10 9 8 7 6 5 4 3 2 1

Library of Congress Cataloging-in-Publication Data

Drouhard, Brianne, 1980-
 Billy the unicorn / by Brianne Drouhard. -- 1st hardcover ed.
    p. cm.
 Summary: Billie the unicorn learns from her cousins that she must be herself to release her true gifts.
 ISBN 978-1-59702-024-4 (hardcover)
 [1. Unicorns--Fiction. 2. Self-confidence--Fiction. 3. Cousins--Fiction.] I. Title.
 PZ7.D818Bi 2011
 [E]--dc22
                2010002435

Billie the Unicorn

By Brianne Drouhard

immedium • San Francisco, CA

Billie the unicorn grew up in a cornfield. There she had spent most of her life, sowing kernels, tending stalks, and playing with corncobs. However, she had decided it was time to visit somewhere new.

Billie remembered the mystical forest where her cousins lived. Rhubarb and Smudge took care of the woods in their own special way. So Billie said good-bye to the place she had called home and set off to find them.

The forest was beautiful and mysterious. Billie couldn't wait to see Rhubarb and Smudge. Strolling in the cool shade and listening to the singing birds, she wondered where her cousins were.

"Billie!" shouted a voice from the shadows.

"Yay! We've missed you!"
Smudge bounded out and gave her a kiss on the nose.

"There is always room in the forest for another unicorn,"
declared Rhubarb, since she loved having company. "I'll put the kettle on."

The three young unicorns had tea, told stories,
and sang songs all night long.

Billie fell asleep, dreaming of all
the adventures tomorrow would bring.

Early the next morning, the three unicorns trotted out to a small clearing in the forest.

Billie watched Smudge playfully
grow enormous sunflowers.
Billie hoped she would learn
how to do the same.

A few skips away,
Rhubarb was adding her own magic
to a patch of strawberries. Humming
a sweet song as she worked, Rhubarb
loved the fruit's scent and Billie did, too.

"It's time for me to practice!" Billie exclaimed with glee. She tried thinking of Rhubarb's strawberries and Smudge's sunflowers.

A small green stem began to curl up from the earth. Billie was excited … what would it be?

It was a corn stalk.

"Wha ha ha!" giggled Smudge. "I've never seen corn grow in the forest before!"

"Smudge, you are being very rude!" Rhubarb scolded her little brother. "Need I remind you when you first tried to grow a flower? It ended up being a mushroom!"

"Billie, don't worry about
what Smudge and I can do,"
advised Rhubarb. "Just be yourself,
think about what you like, and the
magic will do the rest!"

So Billie remembered the clear blue
skies back home, the chubby buzzing
bees, and the smell of the summer wind.

Just then a delicate blue cornflower popped out of the soil.
     "OOOooooh! AHHhhhh!" The cousins were amazed.

"It's so small, but it's very pretty!"
Smudge whispered, as he leaned closer for a good look.

     "Billie, this flower reminds me so much of you!" praised Rhubarb.

Later that afternoon, Billie overheard a conversation.

"Isn't this forest lovely?" hummed the bee. "There are so many swell flowers here!"

"Yes, but I heard the Queen's garden is the most beautiful," quipped the butterfly.

Billie turned to Rhubarb, "Is it true the Queen has the best garden?"

"I don't know, but I am happy staying in the forest. Everything I could ever want is here!" Rhubarb replied with a mouthful of flowers.

But in the days that followed, Billie
continued to wonder what delightful
treasures waited elsewhere.

Then one evening, after dinner and tea,
Billie snuck away from the woods.
She wanted to see the Queen's garden.

Billie thought, "Maybe I could learn more there?" So she headed toward the dark mountains where the Queen's castle lay.

After walking all night, Billie arrived at the Queen's fortress. It rested on top of a great peak and was like nothing she had seen before.

Billie approached the front door, and before she said
a word, the steel gates creaked open. She crept down the
long entryway. Robotic guards stood silently at either side.

"Who comes to visit me?" called a grand
voice from the throne down the hall.

"Um, hi! My name is Billie," the unicorn said nervously. "I heard you have the most beautiful garden. It would be my honor to grow flowers there!"

"Well," sighed the Queen. "Let me see what you can do, and then I shall decide." Billie's horn sparked, and a little blue cornflower sprung from the alabaster floor.

"My, that is quite lovely, isn't it? Well, you must follow me
to the garden." The Queen seemed happy.

"Hooray! I can't wait to tell Rhubarb and Smudge,"
Billie thought, and she proudly followed
the Queen outside.

However, to Billie's surprise, the garden was different from what she had imagined. It was made of large metal flowers. In the middle, sat a weary old unicorn who had been tirelessly creating all the plants around him.

"You can leave now," yawned the Queen, as she removed the old unicorn's chain. "I've found someone to take your place. She is young and will do a better job."

"Now then, show me again what it is you do so well," sneered the Queen coldly.

With a glimmer of magic, another cornflower popped
from the ground. Billie smiled are her tiny creation.

"Ughh, how boring!" complained the Queen.
I've already seen that! Can't you do better?"

"I also know how to grow corn!"
volunteered Billie.
Surely the Queen
must like corn?

"I have no need for corn!"
With that remark, the Queen
smashed the poor little
flower with her scepter.

"Make flowers that look like all the rest," commanded the Queen angrily. "I have a prince visiting tonight, and this garden must look it's best for my guest. You have until sunset!"

Before she stormed away, she chained Billie so she could not leave.

Desperately, Billie tried to do what the Queen wanted. But none of the
flowers turned out right. They were all bent and smelled oddly of corn.
As the hours passed away, Billie did not know what to do.
The only thing left was to cry.

"Billie!" a familiar voice called.

It was Rhubarb! Her friends had climbed up over the stone walls, and now leaped down to their sad cousin. "We've been so worried about you!" Smudge cried. "We're here to take you home."

"I can't go back with you," sobbed Billie. "I am stuck here until I finish the Queen's garden. If I don't, who knows what will happen to me?"

"I know this much: You cannot grow real flowers if you are unhappy,"
decided Rhubarb. "Come on Smudge, let's get to work!"

The two siblings danced circles around the yard. Instantly vines spread
and flowers blossomed. Seeing the bright colors and love of her family,
Billie began to feel much better.

When Rhubarb and Smudge were finished, the place was full of charm
and life. The sun began to set, and soon the Queen strolled in with the prince,
"This is my garden, the most lovely in all the land!" She stopped when she
noticed all the strange plants the little unicorns had grown.

"This is not what I wanted!" she screamed. "These flowers are terri-…"

"Terrific!" exclaimed the prince.

"Oh, thank you, my dear!" the Queen answered slyly. "My hard work was worth it!"

"That's not true!" cried Billie. "My cousins made all of this, not you!"

"I am calling the guards, and your cousins can take your place!" shrieked the Queen.

"We are going home where we belong!" snorted Billie. Her horn began to glow and the earth began to shake.

Suddenly plants sprang beneath the Queen's feet!

The flowers grew as tall as trees, and Billie and her cousins escaped over the castle's walls. "I order you to come back down here!" demanded the Queen.

But her robots could not move— the vines and leaves tangled up their gears. The unicorns headed for their forest home and didn't look back.

Billie thanked her cousins for their help.
"I am sorry for the trouble I've caused.
I'm glad you came to find me. Without
you nothing turned out right, because
my heart was with you the whole time."

The three unicorns went back to their carefree days in the forest. Sometimes on a clear day, they would gaze out at places beyond.

There in the distance, on top of a great mountain, would sit a grand garden, said by many to be the most beautiful in all the land.